D0010236

A Giant First-Start Reader

This easy reader contains only 48 different words,
repeated often to help the young reader develop
word recognition and interest in reading.

Basic word list for *Umbrella Parade*

an	her	parade
and	here	pink
away	him	Pinky
blue	his	Pinky's
can	I	raining
comes	is	red
Dinky	it	today
Dinky's	keep	too
drip	me	umbrella
dry	Molly	umbrellas
fun	Molly's	very
go	my	we
green	need	what
hard	Ollie	will
has	Ollie's	with
have	our	yellow

Umbrella Parade

Written by Kathy Feczko

Illustrated by Deborah Colvin Borgo

Troll Associates

Library of Congress Cataloging in Publication Data

Feczko, Kathy.
    Umbrella parade.

    Summary: Each animal uses a different colored umbrella
while walking in the rain.
    1. Children's stories, American. [1. Umbrellas and
parasols—Fiction. 2. Animals—Fiction. 3. Color—
Fiction] I. Borgo, Deborah Colvin, ill. II. Title.
PZ7.F2985Um   1985   [E]   84-8650
ISBN 0-8167-0356-6 (lib. bdg.)

Copyright © 1985 by Troll Associates, Mahwah, New Jersey
All rights reserved. No part of this book may be used
or reproduced in any manner whatsoever without written
permission from the publisher.
Printed in the United States of America

10 9 8 7 6 5 4 3 2 1

Drip, drip, drip.

It is raining very hard.

I will need my umbrella today.

My red umbrella will keep me dry.

Away I go with my red umbrella.

Here comes Ollie.

Ollie has an umbrella, too.

His umbrella is blue.

Ollie's umbrella will keep him dry.

Away we go with our red and blue umbrellas.

Here comes Molly.

Molly has an umbrella, too.
Her umbrella is yellow.

Molly's yellow umbrella will keep her dry.

Away we go with our red, blue, and yellow umbrellas.

Here comes Pinky.

Pinky has an umbrella, too.

His umbrella is pink.
Pinky's umbrella will keep him dry.

Away we go with our red, blue, yellow, and pink umbrellas.

Here comes Dinky.

Dinky has an umbrella, too.

His umbrella is green.

Dinky's green umbrella will keep him dry.

Away we go with our red, blue, yellow, pink, and green umbrellas.

We can have an umbrella parade!

Drip, drip, drip!

What fun!